Draw
Inspire
Create

First published by Parragon in 2012

Parragon
Chartist House
15-17 Trim Street
Bath BA1 1HA, UK
www.parragon.com

Designed by Talking Design
Illustrations by Eleanor Carter
Written by Frances Prior-Reeves

ISBN 978-1-4454-7241-6
Printed in China

Parragon

Bath • New York • Singapore • Hong Kong • Cologne • Delhi
Melbourne • Amsterdam • Johannesburg • Auckland • Shenzhen

"There is

in seeing what

texture and tone

produce merely

and a bottle of

something magical you can do; what and color you can with a pen point ink."

Ida Rentoul Outhwaite.

y

Fill this page with circles.

Can you see a pattern within your image?

Fill this page with **SQUARES.**
How is your pattern different?

Fill these pages with your

doodles.

Space for your

creativity.

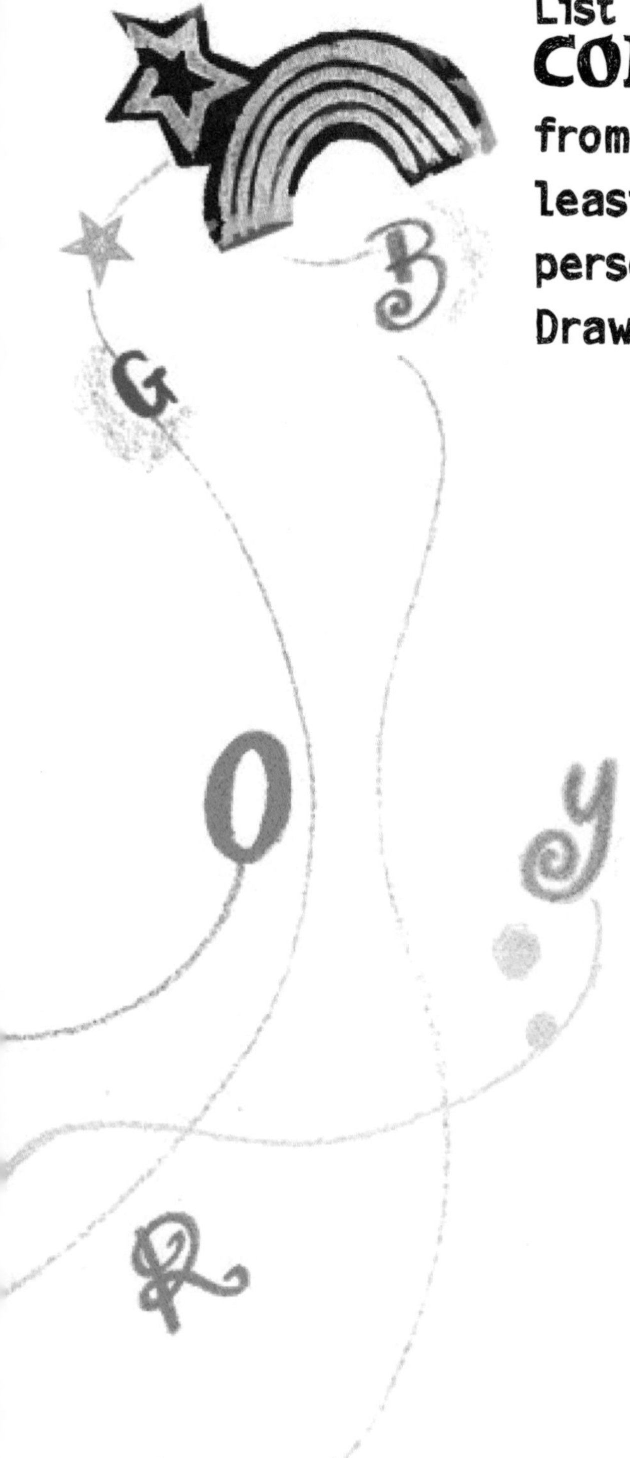

List the **SEVEN COLORS** of the rainbow from your favorite to your least favorite. What does your personal rainbow look like? Draw it.

Red,
Orange,
Yellow,
Green,
Blue,
Indigo,
Violet.

Shade these pages and then use an eraser to cut lines through it.

Create your own **paisley** pattern.

"Color is my obsession, joy,

day-long
and torment."

Claude Monet.

Draw without

RESTRICTIONS.

Play with spiralling lines.

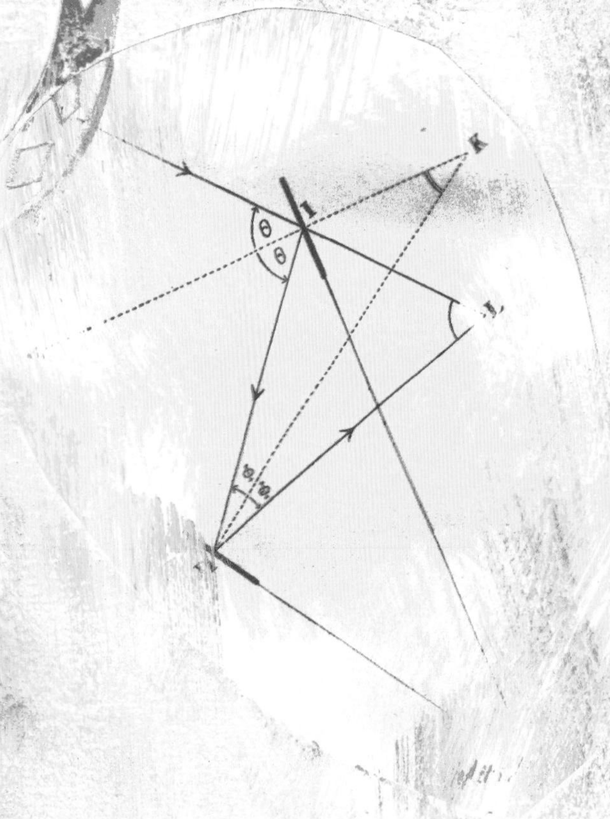

Slice the page with DIAGONAL lines.

Try drawing just wavy lines.

Experiment with ZIGZAGGED lines.

SKETCH!

Pick a **color.**

Look around and draw what you see of that color.

Create a pattern using symbols from your

COMPUTER KEYBOARD.

COLOR these pages.

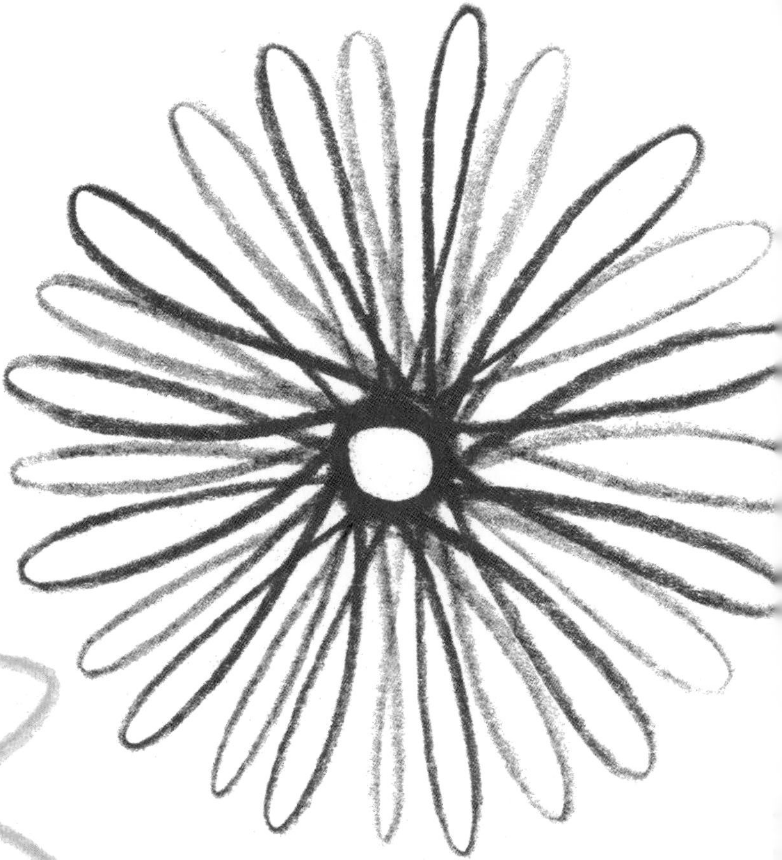

Doodle!

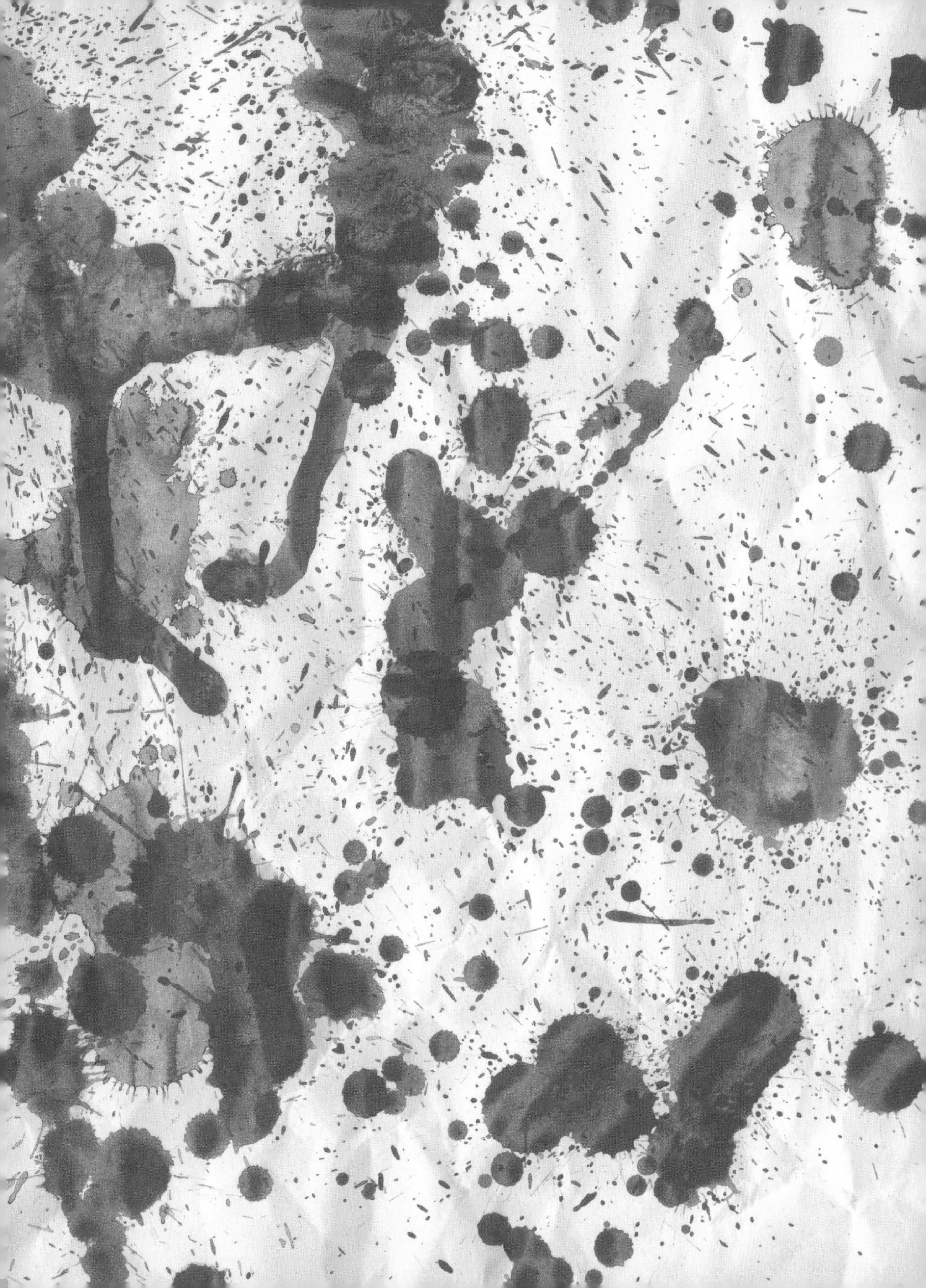

Fill these pages with music...

Using this graph paper create a **MOSAIC** using as many colors as you can.

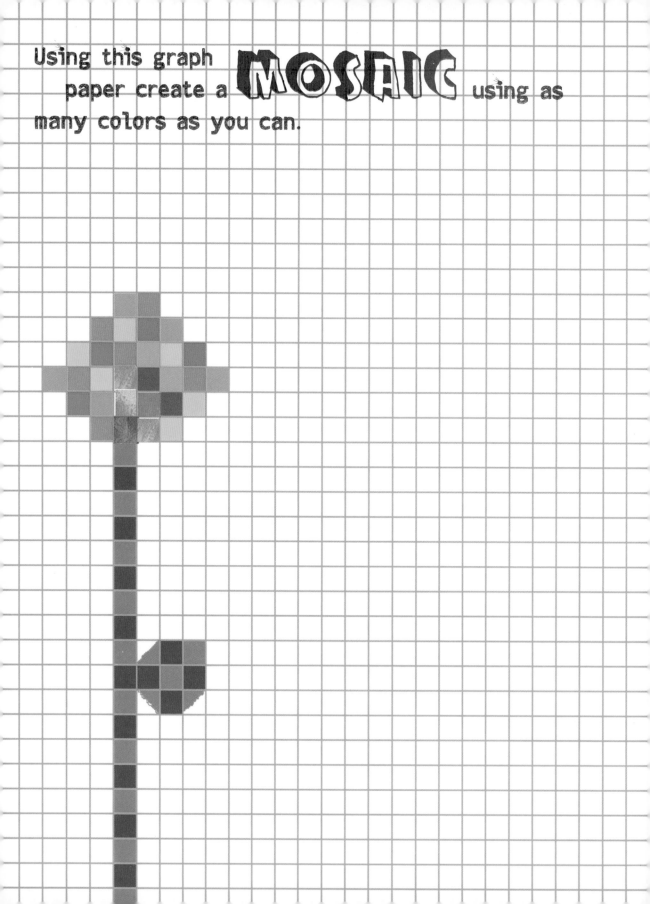

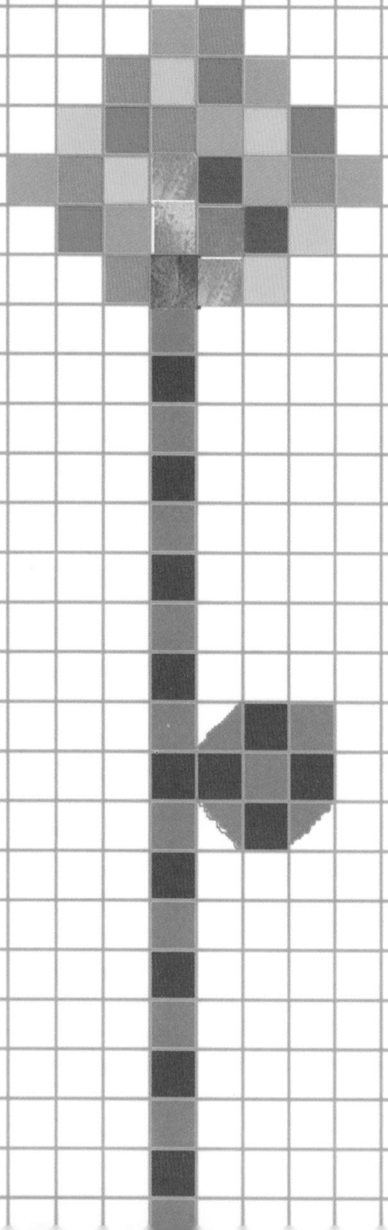

Create a list of words about wood.

Carve those words into a wood grain image.

Eleanor
Eleanor.
Eleanor
ELEANOR
eleanor
eleanor
Eleanor
ELEANOR

Write your **name** over and over, in different **STYLES** and **SIZES**, does it become anything different?

Don't think, just draw.

Draw something secret, then **cut it out** and hide it.

Using a single line draw a SKYLINE.

"I PAINT OBJECTS AS I THINK THEM, NOT AS I SEE THEM."

Pablo Picasso.

Draw different shapes from your

imagination.

Draw something
that begins with
the letter

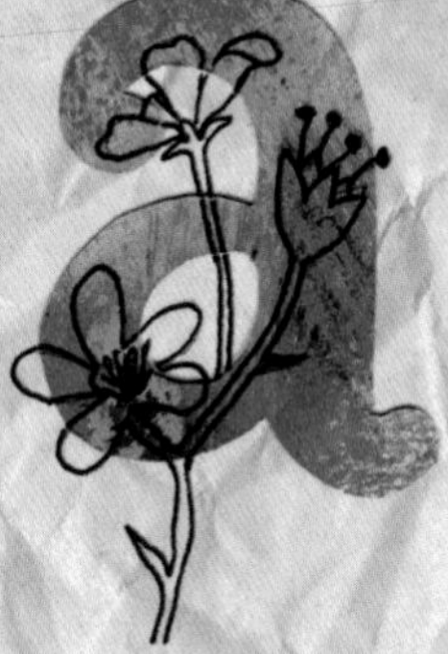

Draw something
that begins
with the letter

Sketch anything.

Your space.

Fill these pages with

birds in flight.

Fill this **TREE** with leaves and life.

Draw a picture of your favorite things in only your **favorite color.**

Draw some

monsters.

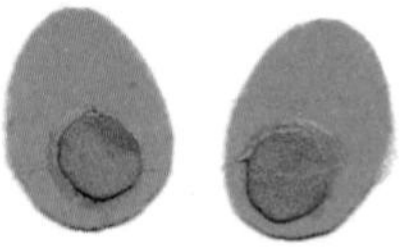

There are no limits.

Draw something TALL.

Draw something small.

a cati pillar

In PRIMARY COLORS only, draw the view from your window.

Draw!

Unleash your creativity on these pages.

Draw a **night sky.**

Draw the last thing you read.

"You can't depend on your eyes when your imagination is out of focus."

Mark Twain.

Fill these pages with **doodles...**

can you do it without taking your pencil off the page?

THINK OUTSIDE THE
BOX AND COLOR
OUTSIDE THE LINES.

Draw a self-portrait using only **ZIGZAGGED** lines.

"There are no only areas against

lines in nature, of color, one another." Edouard Manet.

Draw a *thunderstorm.*

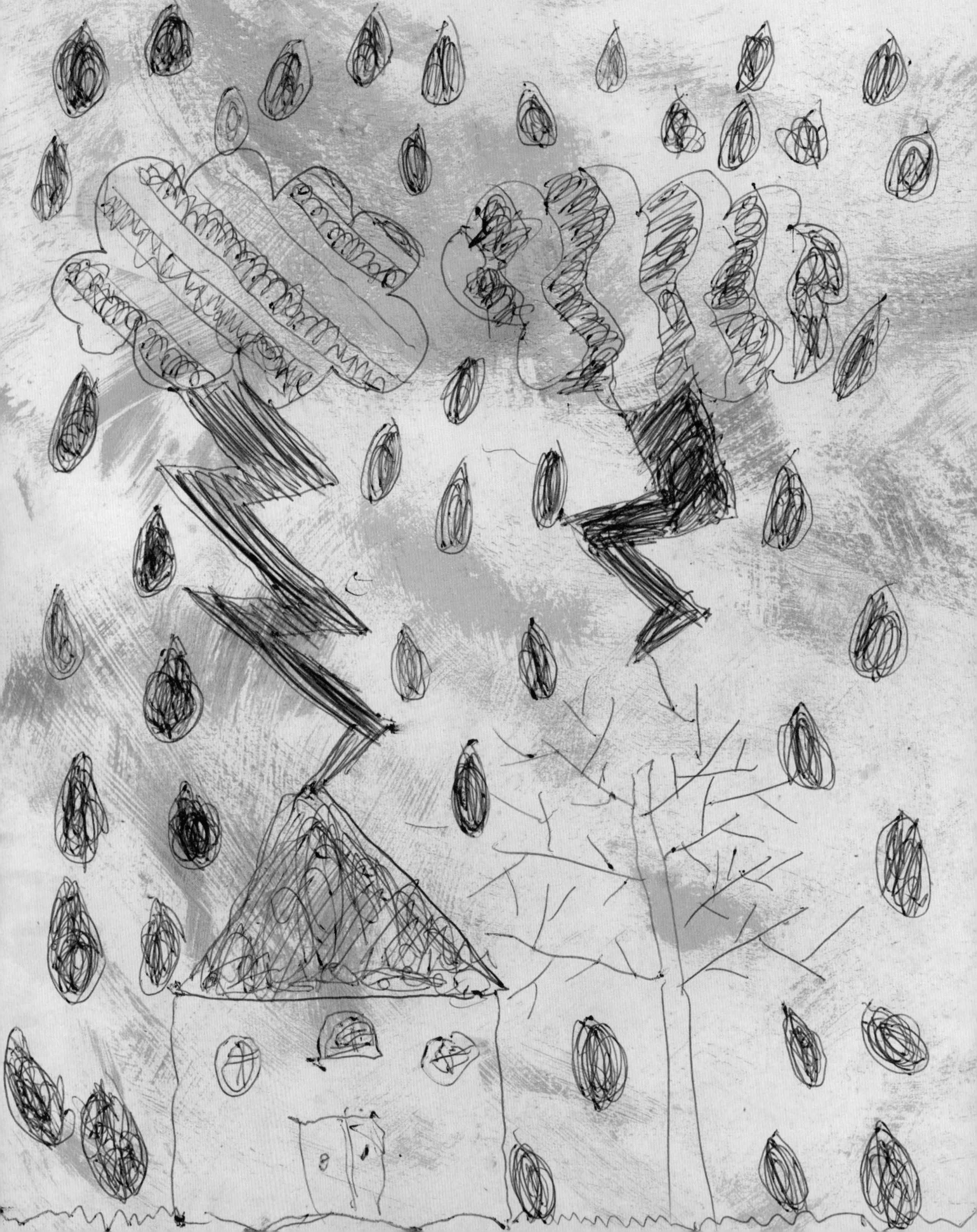

Draw something **furry.**

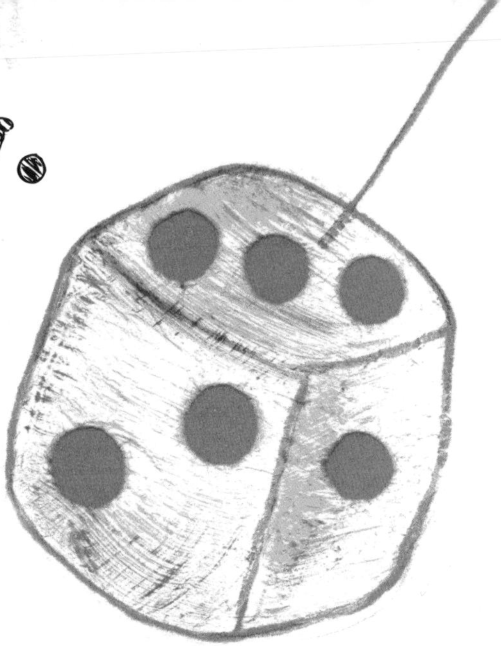

Draw an **animal** using only spiralling lines.

produces

Create!

Using black tones only, draw a **FLOWER GARDEN.**

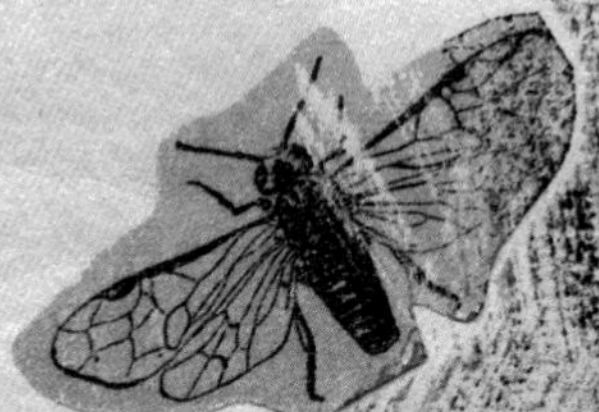

reversed

inverted

upside down

T T T T T T

Using only letters, create a pattern.

inside out

back to front

Create a *list of words* about water.

SUBMERGE those words into an ocean image.

Draw your *mood* using shapes only.

Draw an

angry color.

Draw a **fight** between two colors.

Draw a **brawl** between four colors.

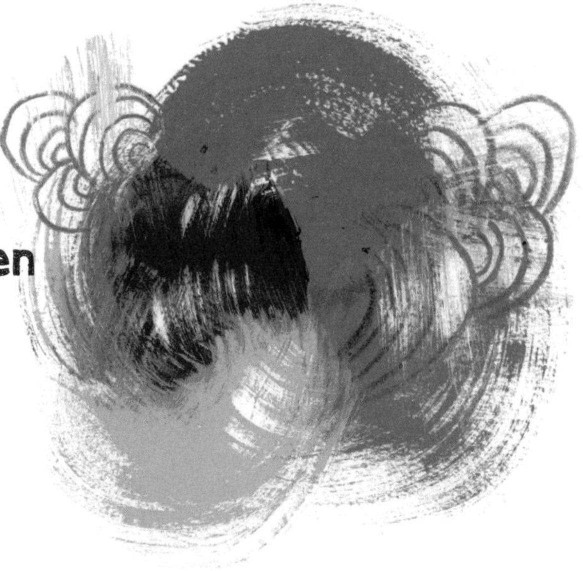

Draw the inside of your house from the outside.

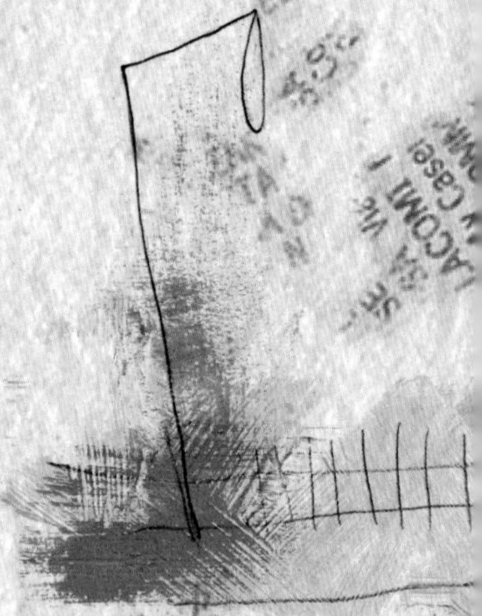

Draw, Paint
Sketch, Doodle
COLOR

Shade
Outline, Depict
Illustrate
Scribble, Jot

DOODLE in or over the gridlines.

Doodles don't have to be mindless.

A
HB

CREATE ANYTHING!

Draw your hand using only

diagonal lines.

Draw a whirlpool of color.

Draw a self-portrait from memory.

Draw a *self-portrait* using a mirror.

Create a **pattern** using only stars.

Personalize this space.

Doodle without taking your pen off the paper.

Try again in a different color.

And again?

"Even if you can't draw, do a little doodle or rip an illustration from a magazine. These visuals will help bring your idea to life."

John Emmerling.

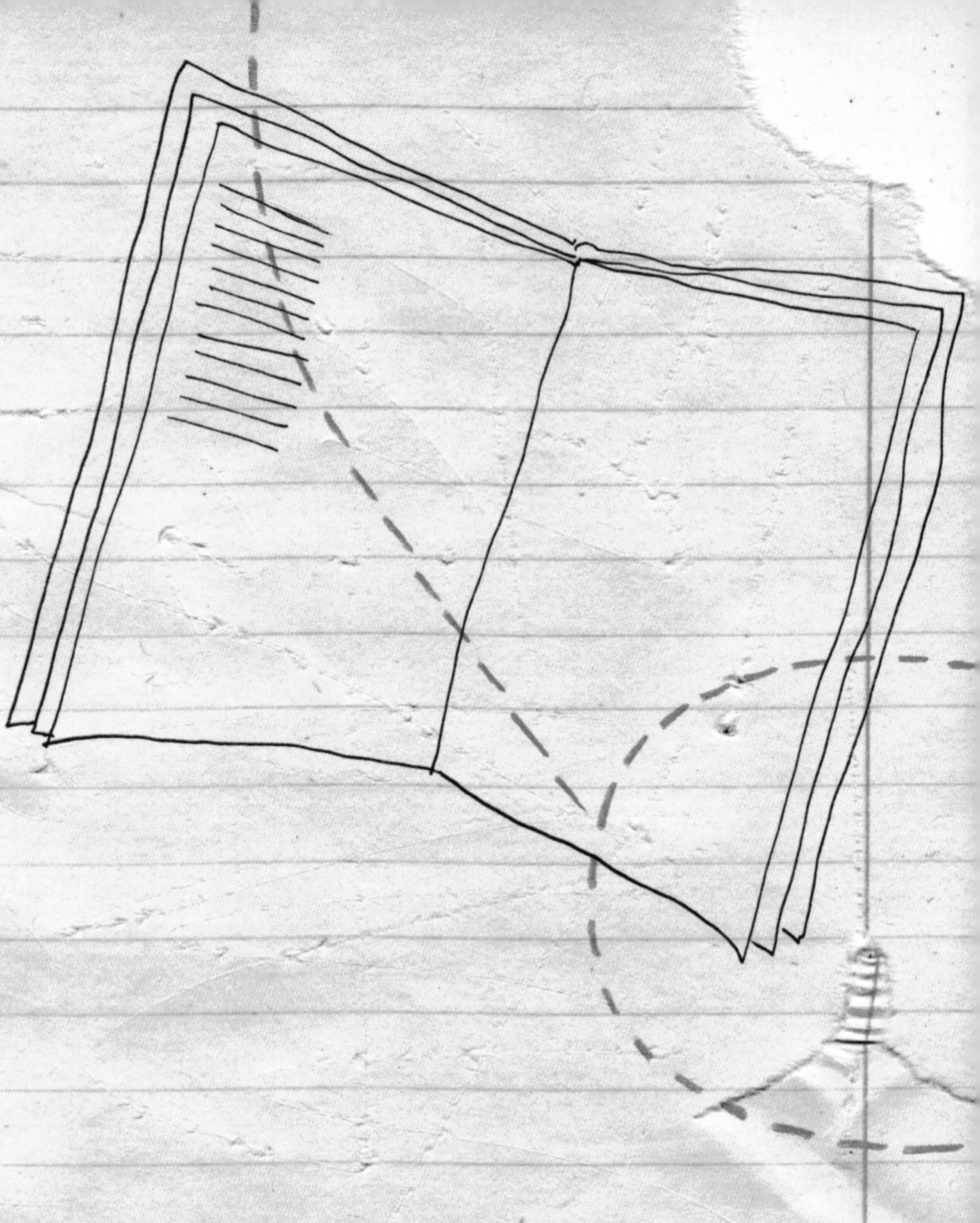

Fill these pages with

DIAMONDS.

Draw fireworks.

Graffiti these pages.

Draw your home using only

wavy lines.

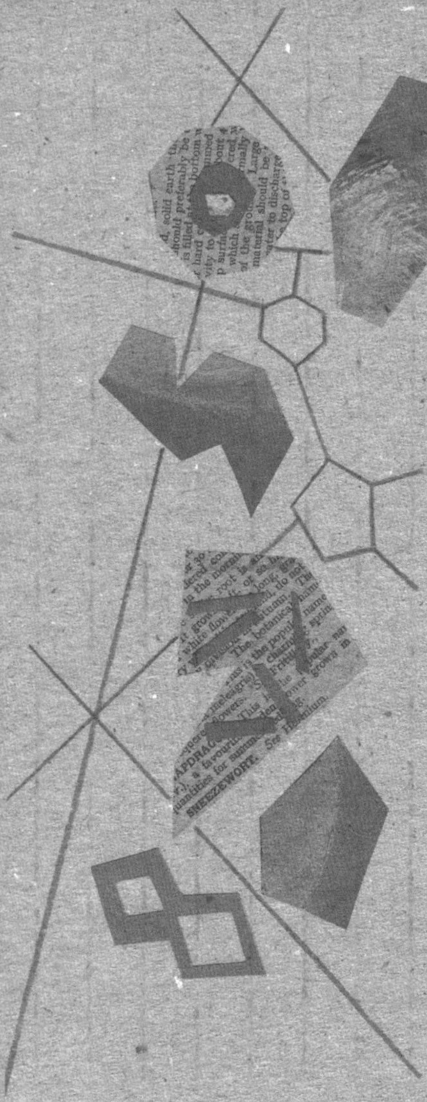

Fill these pages

with **SHAPES** that have

more than four sides.

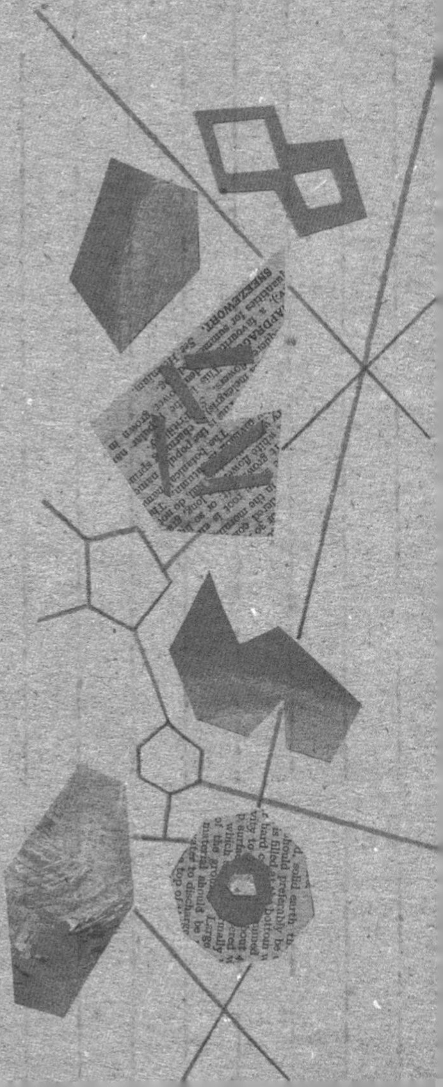

Draw the view of a room as seen through a

KEYHOLE.

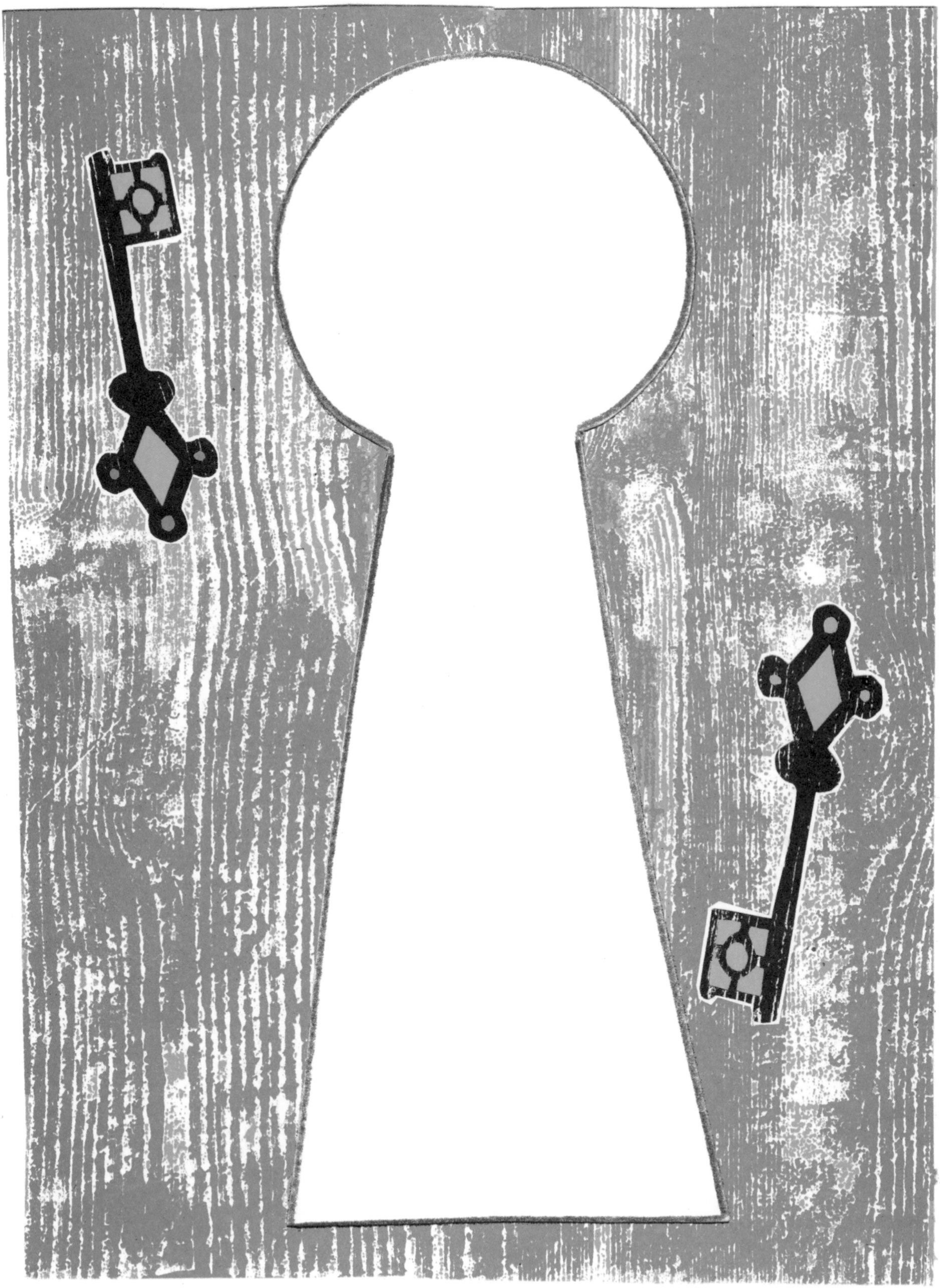

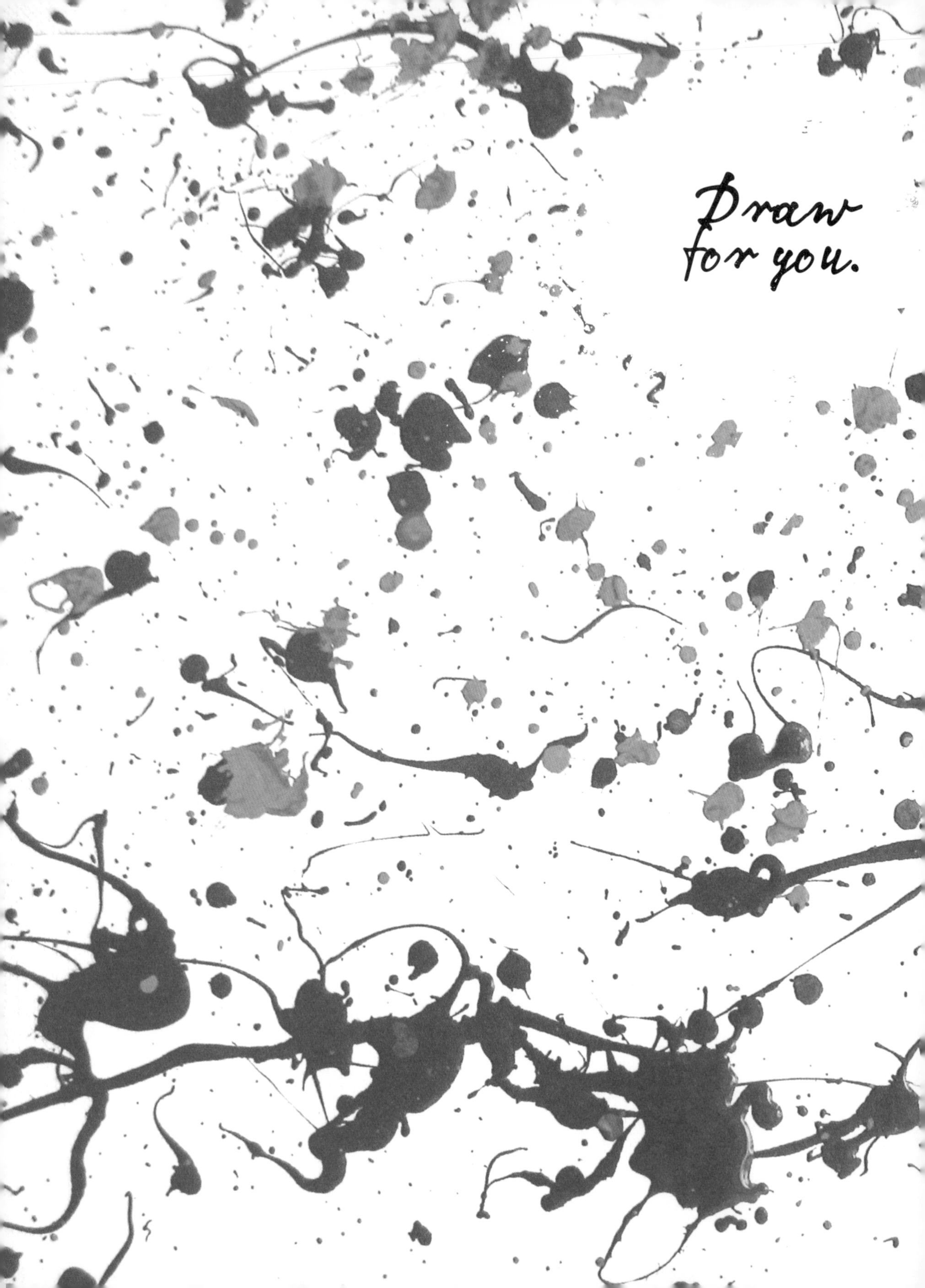
Draw
for you.

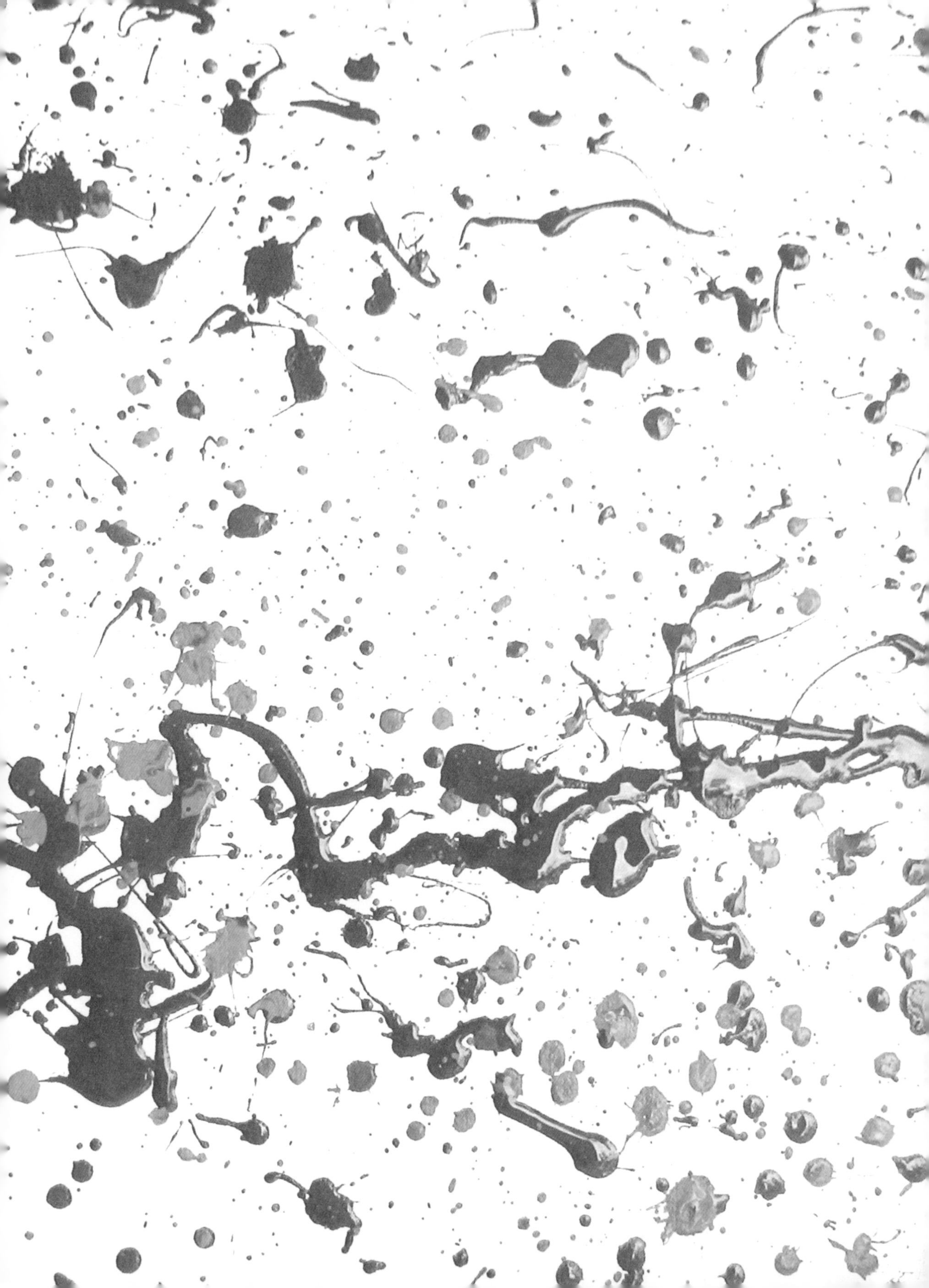

any suc
vacant s
can be
cut bac
their pr
March.
hausted branches can be
or additional branches
Short side growths should
untouched.
Fruiting spurs are kept
cutting back their new
annually,
stopping
nuts, of cou
inwards shoul
so that the bush
centre. Weakly a
and any sucker g
should be remo
trees are pruned similarly. A clos
planted nut hedge will not be
to the same extent, but the sa
pruning princ
lowed.
The ideal bush tree carries
main framework of eight or
branches on a single stem of 12
to 15 in. in le
is trained to the
the manner explained fo
apples in the section H
PROPAGATE F
BUSH
ing

Fill these pages with **smoke.**

SCRIBBLE!

Fill these pages with

spirals.

Draw your mood.

LOVE, SUBMISSION
REMORSE, CONTEM
OPTIMISM, SERE
APPREHENSION
PENSIVENESS, BOR
INTEREST, JO
SURPRISE, SADNES
ANTICIPATION, ECS
TERROR, AMAZEME
RAGE, V

WE, DISAPPROVAL,

, AGGRESSIVENESS,

TY, ACCEPTANCE,

DISTRACTION,

OM, ANNOYANCE,

TRUST, FEAR,

DISGUST, ANGER,

ASY, ADMIRATION,

, GRIEF, LOATHING,

LANCE.

Draw something coming out of this hole.

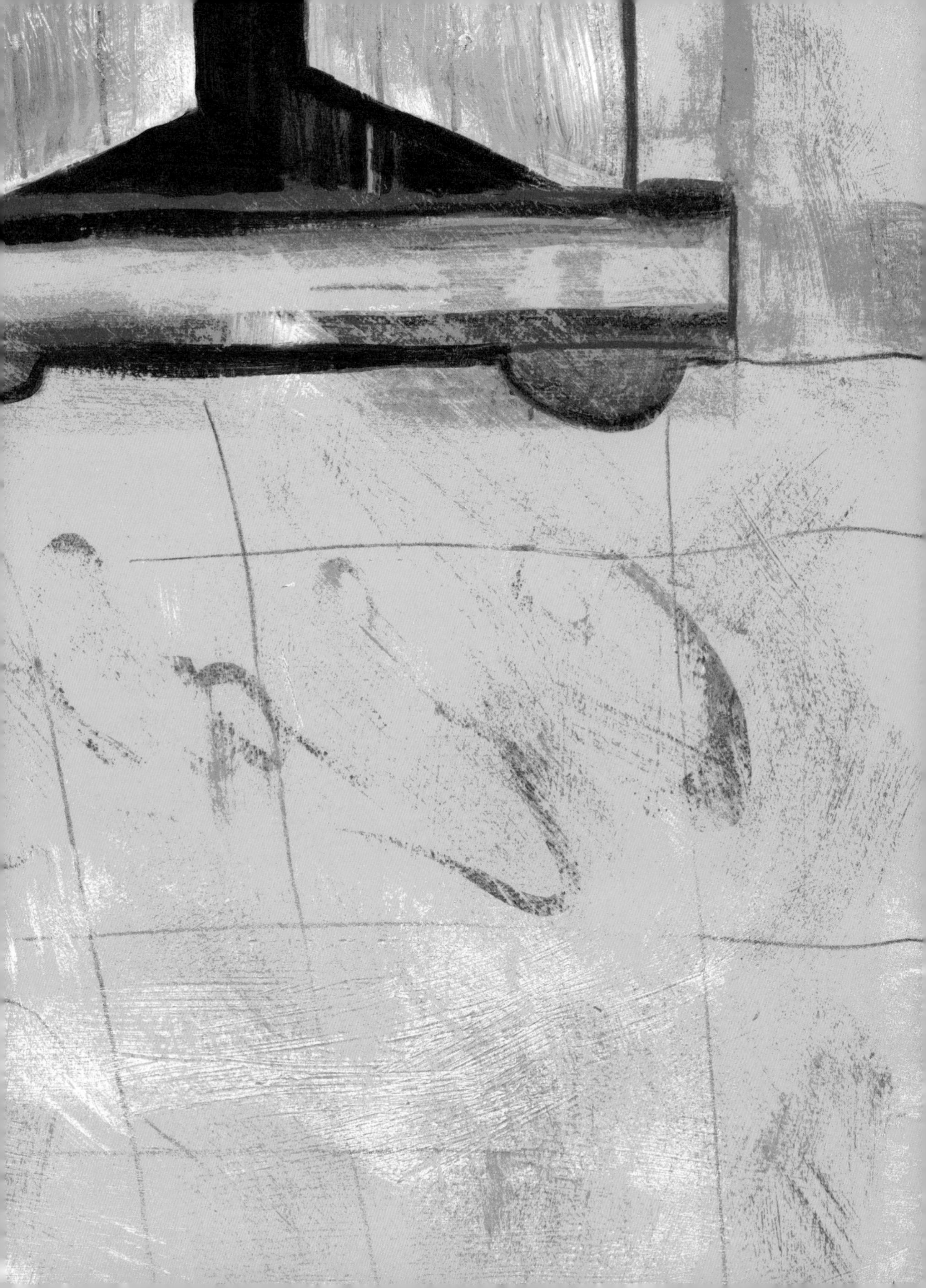

INSPIRE

YOURSELF.

"A Belle To Remember"

Get out, your so old. Your
out, I'm cold. You've got me
untied. I'm in a beehive.
I'm buzzing. Stinging, wanting. how sweet.
Begin a new flee. Your moves - are off-beat.
I'm tryna - get by. I'm in a - beehive. I'm wanting -
feelings - you once had - for me. So go ahead, break my
heart! You'll keep hearing me from afar. Cause I'm a
belle to remember! Do you Remember? A belle to remem
(YOU'LL WANT TO LOVE ME) Belle to remember. Do you remember
A belle to remember. (YOU'LL WANT TO LOVE ME) Mmm
Rebound - you might have. The girls wont match. I'm
tryna get by. I [illegible] cant leave your mind. I'm swimming in your
wanting (from me). To bad - its your loss. You left me undone
You said youre - goodbye. I've left my - beehive. I'm searching
living - Wanting - some peace. Cause - I'm a belle to remember. (YOU'LL WANT TO LOVE
Do you remember? A belle to remember. (YOU'LL WANT TO LOVE
ME) - Belle to remember. Do you remember? A belle to
remember. (YOU'LL WANT TO LOVE ME) - Belle to remember
Do you remember? A belle to remember. (YOU'LL WANT
LOVE ME) Belle to remember. Do you remember? A
belle to remember. (YOU'LL WANT TO LOVE ME) Mm
mm - GO AHEAD and BREAK MY HEART - GO
AHEAD & BREAK MY Heart mm
mmmm Mmm Cause I'm a
Belle to Remember. Do you
remember? A belle to remember
(YOU'LL WANT TO LOVE ME) Belle to
remember mmm I'm a Belle to
remember. Do you remember? A belle to remember
(YOU'LL WANT TO LOVE ME) Go Ahead & break my
heart ~ Go ahead & break my heart mm

Draw your **favorite song.**

Draw the **SOUNDS** coming from this orchestra.

Fill these pages with

IDEAS.

"Creativity is allowing yourself to make mistakes. Art is knowing which ones to keep." Scott Adams.